Angelina Ballerina
Cupcake

Based on the stories by Katharine Holabird
Based on the illustrations by Helen Craig

Ready-to-Read

Simon Spotlight
New York   London   Toronto   Sydney   New Delhi

SIMON SPOTLIGHT

An imprint of Simon & Schuster Children's Publishing Division

1230 Avenue of the Americas, New York, New York 10020

This Simon Spotlight edition December 2020

© 2020 Helen Craig Ltd. and Katharine Holabird. The Angelina Ballerina name and character and the dancing Angelina logo are trademarks of HIT Entertainment Limited, Katharine Holabird, and Helen Craig.

Illustrated by Mike Deas

SIMON SPOTLIGHT, READY-TO-READ, and colophon are registered trademarks of Simon & Schuster, Inc.

For information about special discounts for bulk purchases, please contact Simon & Schuster Special Sales at 1-866-506-1949 or business@simonandschuster.com.

Manufactured in the United States of America 1020 LAK

10 9 8 7 6 5 4 3 2 1

ISBN 978-1-5344-8062-9 (hc)

ISBN 978-1-5344-8061-2 (pbk)

ISBN 978-1-5344-8063-6 (eBook)

CHIPPING CHEDDAR

BAKING CONTEST

COMING SOON!

the flyer said.

Angelina was skipping hom[e]
from ballet class when she
spotted a flyer in
the village square.

Angelina was excited.
She loved to bake
with her mom!

When she got home,
Angelina and her mom
looked at yummy recipes.

They decided to make
delicious Berry Ballerina
cupcakes!

The next day,
Angelina and her mom
went to the market.

Angelina picked out the
freshest strawberries.
Mrs. Mouseling bought
flour, butter, and sugar.

Angelina could not
wait to start baking!

Angelina collected her baking tools.

Just then her sister, Polly,
came into the kitchen.

"Polly, would you like
to help?" Angelina asked.
Polly nodded happily.

Angelina mixed the eggs,
while Polly mixed
the sugar and flour.

They added
the berries together.
Soon the cupcakes were
ready to go in the oven.

Their mom put the cupcakes in the oven while the girls practiced their twirls.

"Oh no!" Angelina said.
She realized they had
forgotten to buy
ingredients for icing!

"My cupcakes will not be Berry Ballerina without icing or decorations!"

"You tried your best,
and that is what matters,"
Angelina's mom said.
Then her mom had an idea.

A few minutes later,
Alice arrived.
She had come to help
her best friend, Angelina!

"We can decorate
the cupcakes
with these pretty
pink ribbons!"
Alice said.

Soon it was time
to head to the contest.

Everything looked yummy!
Dr. Tuttle had made
cheesy cheddar scones.
Miss Quaver had baked her
famous chocolate piano pies.

The judges came by
to try each entry.
Soon they picked a winner.

"The winner of the Chipping Cheddar Baking Contest is . . . Miss Quaver!" a judge announced.

Angelina was disappointed,
but she had a great time
baking with her family
and best friend.

Angelina invited her
friends to a
cupcake party.
What a perfect way to
end the day!